BULLIES AND THE BEAST

First published in 2014 by Wayland

Wayland
338 Euston Road
London NW1 3BH

Wayland Australia
Level 17/207 Kent Street
Sydney, NSW 2000

Consultant: Dee Reid
Editor: Nicola Edwards
Designer: Alyssa Peacock

A CIP catalogue record for this book is available from the British Library.

Bullies and the beast. – (Freestylers data beast; 2)
823.9'2-dc23

ISBN: 978 0 7502 8229 1
E-book ISBN: 978 0 7502 8814 9

Printed in China

Wayland is a division of Hachette Children's Books,
an Hachette UK Company
www.hachette.co.uk

Freestylers

BULLIES AND THE BEAST

Andrew Fusek Peters

and Alex McArdell

WAYLAND

www.waylandbooks.co.uk

Titles in the series

Bats!

978 0 7502 8231 4

Bullies and the Beast

978 0 7502 8229 1

Monster Savings

978 0 7502 8232 1

Poison!

978 0 7502 8230 7

CHAPTER 1

It was after school and I was watching Roz tapping away at the computer.

"You really think you can hack into the computers of those big companies?" I asked her.

"Hey, Kiran, I was born to hack!" joked Roz.

"Those big companies don't care if they pollute our planet," said Roz.

"So I am going to hack into their computers and show how they are cheating on their taxes."

There was a sudden groan.

"What was that?" I asked.

"Don't know," replied Roz. "Something strange is going on."

"You're right," I said. "It looks like smoke coming out of the screen!"

We both stared at the screen.

As we watched the lines of numbers started to change.

They began to swirl around.

Then they began to form an image.

"That's so strange," said Roz. "It looks like a ..."

We both said it at once:

"... Monster!"

The numbers on the screen had formed into a giant 3D scary monster.

Roz laughed. "One of my hacking mates must be playing a trick on me," she said.

But that did not explain how the swirling screen monster turned real!

Huge hands shot out of the screen.

The hands were glowing, as if they were made out of hard disks and motherboards. The nails were as sharp as swords. It wasn't an image any more. It was alive.

"This is no trick," I shouted. "What have you done?"

"I don't know," said Roz quietly. "I have no idea what's going on."

I knew we should run, but we couldn't. The sight of this computer beast was amazing and terrible. The groaning sound was getting louder. Then the hand stretched towards Roz, trying to strangle her.

"Hun... Hung... Hungry!" groaned the beast. "Need. Eat. Now."

CHAPTER 2

"I've got some peanuts!" said Roz and she quickly reached inside her bag.

"Here you go," she said shoving the peanuts at the beast.

But the beast's hand brushed the peanuts aside.

I looked at the screen again. It wasn't just hands now. There were arms and a huge body. The monster squeezed right out of the computer. It stood towering over us... I thought I was going to puke with fear.

"Heed numbers," the beast said. It buzzed like electric wasps.

"You mean like this?" asked Roz and she pulled out her calculator and handed it over.

The beast grabbed the calculator and crunched it up like cornflakes. Then the beast began to glow.

"What do we do with him?" hissed Roz.

"I don't know!" I said. "You made him. You get rid of him."

Then the beast made a sudden leap towards the window.

"Look!" it buzzed. "Bad one!"

I ran over to the window. In the park outside, a bunch of BMX boys hung out on the ramps.

One of the boys had chucked his crisp packet on the ground. Nothing new there. Our park was a tip most of the time.

Before we could stop him the beast had opened the window and jumped out. He had also changed shape. Now he was racing over the grass like a huge wolf.

"Not good!" said Roz, as we both climbed out to catch him.

By the time we got there, the boy was shaking like a leaf.

"Call off your mad dog," he squeaked.

"Eat rubbish," growled the beast.

"What?" said the boy. His mates backed away.

Roz understood the beast's words. "Eat the rubbish," she repeated.

"You're mad," said the boy. "I'll call the police."

"If you don't do as it says, Fido will attack you," I said to the boy.

Slowly the boy picked up the crisp packet and stuck it in his mouth.

Roz smiled at me. Maybe a computer beast was not all bad news!

CHAPTER 3

"Well done, Fido!" I shouted as the three of us ran out of the park.

"I don't think he'll chuck a crisp packet on the ground again in a hurry," said Roz.

"Did well? Yes?" the beast growled.

"Oh yeah," said Roz. "But we've got to get off home now and we can't take you with us."

I thought for a moment.

"I've got an idea," I said. "The school has a back-up server room. It's full of machines and numbers for Fido to eat. It's the perfect place for him to spend the night."

"Good idea!" said Roz. "Sometimes you really surprise me."

I tried not to blush. It didn't solve the monster problem, but it was a start.

The next day started badly. With all the fun of the night before, I hadn't done my homework. As I was being told off, I heard sniggering behind me. It was Chelsea, Kylie and Kayley. They were the real monsters in our school. They left me alone. But they liked to pick on Roz.

"Alright nerd?" said Kayley. "Have you met any boyfriends on that computer of yours?"

Roz ignored them. But then Chelsea joined in.

"You have to be one of the most boring girls in the universe," she said.

"Leave her alone!" I said.

"Leave her alone, or what?" sneered Kylie. "You will start a fight?" She flashed her nails in front of my face.

"These are sharp enough to take your eyes out," she threatened. "So crawl back into your hole like a good mouse."

"You know what?" said Roz. "You lot really hack me off. Why don't we have it out? In the park. Six o'clock tonight. That's if you're not scared."

"Ooohhhh!" they all sneered. "We're so terrified."

"You will regret taking us on," said Chelsea and she, Kylie and Kayley stormed off.

"What did you do that for?" I said. "They will beat us to a pulp!"

"Ah!" said Roz with a smile. "You forgot we have a new friend!"

CHAPTER 4

It was after school. Roz and I were heading round the back of the I.T. block. We were going to check up on the monster.

"I've been thinking," I said.

"Never a good idea," joked Roz.

"No, listen to me," I said. "We don't know what that thing could do."

"Think about it," I told her. "You punched a few keys and made a beast out of thin air. Doesn't that worry you?"

"Yes and no," said Roz. "I wanted to do something to make a difference. These companies are cheating on their taxes."

"I know they are," I said. "But we are only a couple of teenagers. How can we change the world?"

"Fine," Roz said angrily. "You go home and watch TV. I'm going to do something."

That was the thing with Roz. Either you were in or you were out. I was in.

We were expecting the room with the computer servers to be a mess. But there was the beast, curled up like a giant bear on the floor. Snoring. It was almost sweet, apart from the fact that he was a monster.

"Wakey wakey, Fido!" I shouted.

The huge beast opened one eye and then closed it again. The groaning voice said, "I am... not hungry."

I gave the monster a gentle prod.

It opened both eyes. It sniffed the air and looked round.

"What if it thinks we could be its next snack?" I asked, trying not to tremble.

"Known fact," said Roz. "Monsters never eat their maker."

The beast looked at me. Then it turned to look at Roz. Its big black eyes looked sad.

Then it spoke in a quiet voice.

"What... am... I?"

I felt quite sorry for it.

"I can't really tell you," said Roz. "But I know you have some work to do."

Then she did something bonkers, or very brave. She went up to the beast, and scratched it behind the ear.

Instead of swiping her head off, the beast began to purr.

CHAPTER 5

The park was dark. Standing in the shadows were Chelsea, Kayley and Kylie. They looked even more threatening out of school.

"We don't need any weapons!" Chelsea sneered.

"Just nails and fists," Kayley joined in. "You and your sissy boyfriend will wish you had never crossed us."

"Got any bright ideas?" Roz whispered to me.

"Do what I do," I whispered back.

"Listen," I said. My voice was shaking. "We don't want any trouble. We came here to offer you money to leave us alone."

"That's more like it!" yelled Kylie. "The cowards want to pay us off!"

"Yes," I shouted. "We do want to pay you… to pay you back for all the misery you've caused your victims."

By now, Roz and I were striding straight towards them, all fear gone.

"You're crazy," snarled Kylie. "You don't stand a chance against us."

"Maybe we don't," said Roz. "But we have a friend who doesn't like people polluting the earth with their bullying."

In the darkness, something groaned.

"What was that?" said Chelsea looking around.

"We hacked your laptop," said Roz. "We saw how much nasty stuff you like to spread about people. Say you're sorry now and promise to stop or...."

"Or what?" laughed Kylie. "You two are a joke!"

But the monster that landed in the middle of them was no joke. It gave a roar and the trees around shook.

"Hungry!" it growled. Chelsea began to cry as her mates clung to her.

"We're sorry," sobbed Chelsea. "We promise we won't do anything ever again. Just get that thing away from us!"

"OK," said Roz. "But trust me, if you don't keep your word, you will be seeing our friend again."

The three girls ran for their lives.

Roz and I burst out laughing.

The beast looked at each of us in turn.

"I... did... well. Yes?" it asked.

"You did great," said Roz. "But we can't call you Fido anymore. Respect and that."

"How about Data Beast?" I said.

"I am... Data Beast," said the beast.

"Oh yes you are," said Roz. "And I'm sure you came out of that computer for a reason. I can't wait to see what you'll do next!"

FOR TEACHERS

About Freestylers

Freestylers is a series of carefully levelled stories, especially geared for struggling readers of both sexes. With very low reading age and high interest age, these books are humorous, fun, up-to-the-minute and edgy. Core characters provide familiarity in all of the stories, build confidence and ease pupils from one story through to the next, accelerating reading progress.

Freestylers can be used for both guided and independent reading. To make the most of the books you can:

- Focus on making each reading session successful. Talk about the text before the pupil starts reading. Introduce the characters, the storyline and any unfamiliar vocabulary.

- Encourage the pupil to talk about the book during reading and after reading. How would they have felt if they were Roz? Or Kiran? How would they have reacted to the Data Beast and tackled the bullies?

- Talk about which parts of the story they like best and why.

For guidance, this story has been approximately measured to:

National Curriculum Level: 2A
Reading Age: 8.6
Book Band: White

ATOS: 2.7
Lexile ® Measure [confirmed]: 360L